The Butt Book

Artie Bennett illustrated by **Mike Lester**

BLOOMSBURY

NEW YORK BERLIN LONDON

Published by Bloomsbury U.S.A. Children's Books
175 Fifth Avenue, New York, New York 10010

Library of Congress Cataloging-in-Publication Data
Bennett, Artie.
The butt book / by Artie Bennett ; illustrated by Mike Lester.—1st U.S. ed.
p.   cm.
Summary: In illustrations and rhyming text, celebrates the uses
and varieties of buttocks of all kinds and shapes.
ISBN-13: 978-1-59990-311-8 • ISBN-10: 1-59990-311-3 (hardcover)
ISBN-13: 978-1-59990-456-6 • ISBN-10: 1-59990-456-X (reinforced)
[1. Stories in rhyme. 2. Buttocks—Fiction.] I. Lester, Mike, ill. II. Title.
PZ8.3.B43754Bu 2010   [E]—dc22   2009008707

Art created with scratchboard and watercolor
Typeset in Elroy
Book design by Nicole Gastonguay

First U.S. Edition January 2010
Printed in China by Printplus Limited, Shenzhen, Guangdong
2 4 6 8 10 9 7 5 3 1 (hardcover)
2 4 6 8 10 9 7 5 3 1 (reinforced)

All papers used by Bloomsbury U.S.A. are natural, recyclable products
made from wood grown in well-managed forests. The manufacturing processes
conform to the environmental regulations of the country of origin.

To Leah, my muse —A. B.

To Regan, Hope, and Grady:
my three favorite butts —M. L.

Eyes and ears are much respected,

but the butt has been neglected.

We hope to change that here and now.

Would the butt please take a bow?

Buttocks is the
formal name—
and no two buttocks
are the same.

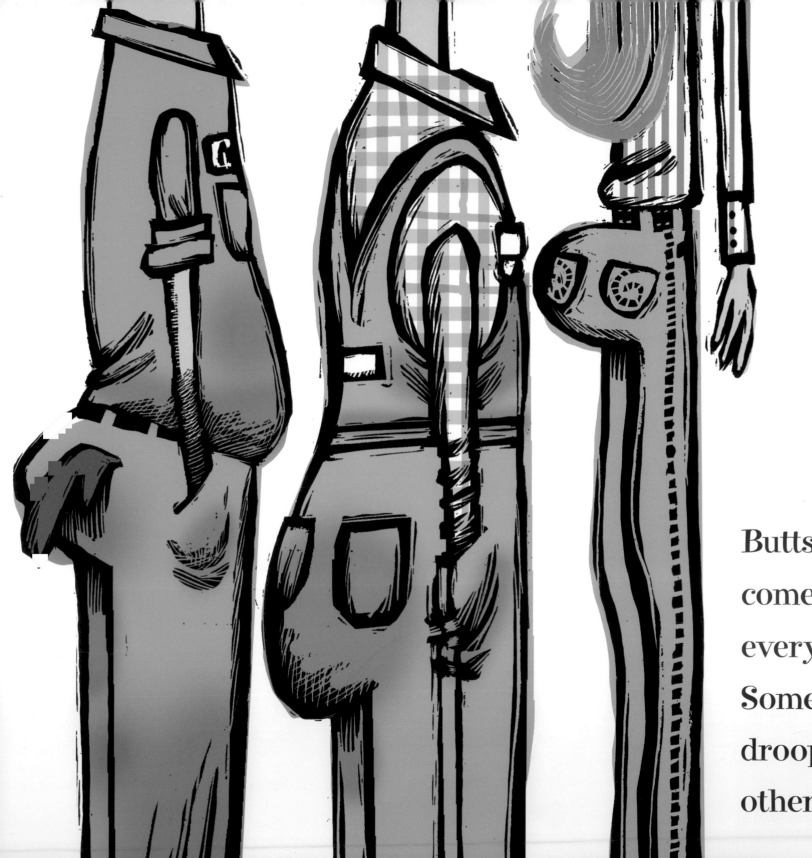

Butts can
come in
every size.
Some will
droop and
others rise.

There are countless shapes of butts;
one may be flat, another juts.

Butts are found across the earth.

We have them from the day of birth.

Some names for butts have foreign flair:

tuchas, keister, derriere!

Fanny, bottom,
heinie, rear—
butts, oh, butts
are back, my dear!

Even mummies,
like King Tut,
have a well-worn,
well-wrapped butt.

Lots of creatures have behinds.

There are just so *many* kinds!

Elephants have
mighty ones,
while hippos have
untidy ones.

Giraffe butts are
supremely tall,

but mouse butts
are extremely
small.

Best in show
or just plain mutt,
every doggy has
a butt.

Patches found on baboon rumps
help them when they sit on stumps.

On their butts, skunks have a gland
that sprays a stink no one can stand.

White on black
or black on white,
the zebra's butt is
out of sight!

A leopard's butt is
sleek and spotted.
Some fish behinds
are polka-dotted!

Snake behinds just don't exist—
something no snake has ever missed.

An eagle's butt
soars high above.

A teddy bear's
is filled with love.

Why do we have butts? Perchance,
a place to place our underpants?

Butts are vital body parts,
important as our heads or hearts.

Our rumps provide a built-in chair
we carry with us everywhere!

When dancing, you can shake your booty.

Shake, shake, shake, you little cutie.

Some exercise
their butts with zeal
in hopes of having
buns of steel.

Without your butt,
you're incomplete.
You could not use
the toilet seat.

Without your butt,
you could not ride
your shiny, brand-new
bike outside.

You could not sit
upon a swing,

a seesaw, or
most anything!

So respect your butt and listen, folks.

It must not be the butt of jokes.

Bottoms up!
Hip, hip, hooray!
Our useful butts
are here to stay.

Don't undercut
your butt, my friend.
Your butt will thank
you in . . .

PonyRides